The Golden Touch

A Greek Myth

Adapted by: Michelle Baron

Lyrics by: Michelle Baron and Phil Baron
Music by: George Wilkins

Illustrated by:

Russell Hicks	Fay Whitemountain
Theresa Mazurek	Su-Zan
Douglas McCarthy	Lisa Souza
Allyn Conley	Julie Ann Armstrong
Lorann Downer	Julie Zakowski
Rivka	Pat Ventura

This Book Belongs To:

Use this symbol to match book and cassette.

nce upon a time, in a beautiful kingdom, King Midas lived with his young daughter, Alizia. Alizia loved to surround herself with beauty. Most of all, she loved the brilliant red roses that grew right in the palace garden.

She always picked flowers for her father and gave them to him at breakfast.

Midas loved the flowers, and he loved his daughter very much. But you see, King Midas had an even greater love…gold. For every morning after breakfast, Midas went into his special room where he surrounded himself with gold.

Page 1

Now on one particular morning, King Midas was especially anxious to see his gold. He skipped breakfast and hurried off to his special room. There Midas sat admiring his gold, chuckling and talking to himself.

Someone spoke.

Midas looked up and saw an old man who had the look of wisdom in his eyes. The old man had come because he heard the sound of laughter. Could it really be that gold brought all this happiness to the king?

"I'm Sold On Gold"

I'm sold on gold!
He's sold on gold!
Let the world be told
I'm sold on gold!

There's something about the weight and the shape,
And the size and the smell,
Oh yes! You can tell
That it's gold! Just think
About that clink! clink! clink!
And I don't have to share it,
My 24 Karat!

Something about the gleam and the sheen,
And the shimmer and the shine,
Oh boy! It's all mine!
Hear that jingle-ling ling?
I'm a happy king!
And it's my royal passion
To love my cash 'n gold.

He's a king who meddles in metals.
I'm nuts for nuggets, aren't you?
I'm a boy who's bonkers for bullion.
He's a fellow who loves yellow–
It's true!

I'm sold on gold!
He's sold on gold!
Let the world be told
I'm sold on gold!

It's a must to have a bit of gold dust!
He's sold on gold!

It seemed to be true. Nothing brought King Midas more happiness than gold.

Then King Midas told the old man of his very special wish…that everything he touched might turn to gold.

The old man asked Midas if he was certain of his wish. Midas assured him that he was. So the old man told Midas that in the morning, with the rising of the sun, he would have his wish…he would have the Golden Touch!

Silently the old man left. But Midas was not sure if the old man meant what he had said.

That night Midas could hardly sleep. Finally he couldn't wait any longer. He got out of bed and dressed himself. Then he looked at his hands.

Carefully King Midas reached for a vase. He touched it, but nothing happened.

But then the old man's
words echoed in his mind… he would have the
Golden Touch in the morning, "with the rising of the sun."

King Midas sat patiently until the first golden rays of sunlight streamed into the room. As soon as they did, he once again reached for the vase. He touched it and…

…the vase actually turned to gold! It shimmered and shined in the beautiful sunlight!

Midas ran around his bedroom touching everything until he was, floor to ceiling, completely surrounded by gold!

King Midas felt more like a king than ever before. But he would soon feel quite differently because, when he tried to eat his breakfast, the food he touched…also turned to gold.

Then Alizia entered the dining room carrying another bouquet of red roses for her father.

King Midas was so relieved to see his daughter that he forgot all about his Golden Touch. He reached out to accept the flowers. And the beautiful red roses turned to gold!

Alizia began to cry because now the roses had lost their beautiful fragrance and color.

The last thing in the world Midas wanted to do was make his daughter unhappy. He tried to apologize to Alizia and he reached out to hold her hands. But when their hands met…

Alizia turned to gold!

Sadly the king leaned over to kiss his daughter's cheek, and as he did, he felt the touch of cold, hard gold.

For a long time King Midas gazed upon the golden teardrop that remained motionless on his daughter's face. Now he realized that her love was worth more to him than all the gold in the world.

Midas knew that he had to undo what he had done. He had to find the old man.

Midas looked all through the city and the countryside, hoping that someone had seen the old man.

Finally someone told King Midas where the old man could be found. And there, just as he was told, at the top of a hill was a cave. And inside the cave, the golden light of a fire burned brightly.

Midas started up the steep path that led to the cave. Suddenly he slipped and fell, turning the path into gold!

It was a hard climb, but eventually Midas was able to reach the top.

There in the cave, next to the crackling golden fire, sat the old man.

Midas told the old man that he had made a drastic mistake. Greed had caused Midas to lose what his heart valued most. He no longer wanted the Golden Touch.

Smiling, the old man told the king to go home and assured him that all would be undone.

As the king hurried down the path, the gold that lay before him disappeared. Everything returned to normal as he passed by.

Before long, Midas stood before his daughter and reached for her hands just as they, too, returned to normal. He bent to kiss her warm cheek.

"The Most Precious Gift"

When you give me a smile
Your eyes are so bright,
They tell me that everything's all right.

And when I kiss your cheek
And when I hold you tight,
Then I give you a gift you can keep through the night.

From parent to child
Or friend to friend,
There is one gift that has no end.
Far greater than gold
Is what I'm thinking of.
The most precious gift
Is the gift of love.

You held my hand
When I walked by your side.
You wiped my tears whenever I cried.
These are the gifts
That gold cannot buy.
You gave them to me without asking why.

From parent to child
Or friend to friend,
There is one gift that has no end.
Far greater than gold
Is what I'm thinking of.
The most precious gift
Is the gift of love.
The gift of love.

King Midas gave his daughter a great big hug. As she hugged him back, Alizia noticed something out of the corner of her eye.

The roses had become beautifully red and fragrant again.

King Midas knew that nothing in the world was as precious as his daughter's love. From that day on, the only gold he cherished was the golden light that shined upon his daughter's hair.

nd they all lived happily ever after.